WHERE HORROR COMES HOME TO ROOST!
EYRIE

22ND SPECTRAL ISSUE!

EYRIE
WHERE HORROR COMES HOME TO ROOST!

Cover: Mike Hoffman **Stories:** Mike Hoffman, Ray Mackay, Barry Buchanan, Juan Alcudia
Artwork: Mike Hoffman, Carlos Lamani

ISSUE 22 JUNE 2024

CONTENTS

The Bloody Baron
In air-battles over the English Channel during World War II a strange and horrible combatant appears to be a winged monster!

Ice in the Veins
A strange passenger boards a doomed ocean liner with two small children, her servant, and an insatiable thirst!

The Last Vampire
In a World where a race of Vampires dominates and feeds upon all others, what may happen if the balance is forever upset?

Vampires of the Old West
An illuminating inquiry into the rumored existence of actual Vampires in the halcyon days of the legendary Old American West.

The Rogues Gallery
A genuinely grisly journey through the infamous and less-than-famous Historical Vampire figures that dot the landscape!

Let the Corpses Lie
In a bygone era of big-city Crime, a lone thief and gun-for-hire stumbles into a strange situation he never could have expected.

The Bloody Baron

The Last Vampire

The Rogues Gallery

Ice in the Veins

Vampires of the Old West

Let the Corpses Lie

EYRIE Issue 22, June 2024 is published by Mike Hoffman, EYRIE is copyright to Mike Hoffman. All rights reserved. No part of this book may be used or reproduced (except for review purposes) without the express written permission of Mike Hoffman. Any resemblance to persons (living or undead!) events, institutions or locales is purely coincidental. First Printing.

THE CHOPPING BLOCK
LETTERS TO EYRIE MAGAZINE

Hi Mike,

What an alluring cover for your special Mermaid issue, I felt like I was right there at the bottom of the sea with those mermaids, and what an added bonus with those fantastic mermaid paintings on the inside front & back covers!

Eyrie has reached a new level and has risen to the top of heap of Horror magazines by far! The first three tales were hard-hitting combustions to my head with "Forever Yours" putting me down for the count! The two one pagers " Tears of Dugong" & "Deep-Sea Fornication Facts" were very interesting and informative. The last three stories were great with "A Date with Destiny in Monster town" giving me a big smile to me face and brought me back to life!

Oh, by the way the art was top notch as usual. Thanks for such an intense reading experience!
Johnny "Wolf Boy" Castiglia

Fangs for your continued support, Wolf-Boy!

Dear Mr. Hoffman,
I just finished reading and loving Eyrie issue twenty! Man, I never knew mermaids could be so scary! Up until now, my only horrifying experience with them was the time my little sister made me watch The Little Mermaid with her!

I was really "blown away" by the nuclear ending to Barry Buchanan's "Darkest Depths" story and like that the story was set in the unique setting of a submarine. It reminded me of "Below", an underrated horror movie I love.

I'd love to see more Eyrie horror stories set in more unique settings and locations! Can't wait to see what you and the Eyrie Magazine Crew come up with next!
Sincerely,
Max Shea, New York City, NY

Thanks Max, we're continuously churnin' away in the dungeons here crankin' out even more quality Terror-Tales for loyal readers such as yourself!

Dear Mike and the Eyrie Cohorts,
First off, lemme just say how totally wicked Eyrie magazine seventeen was! I loved how y'all clearly all started from the same idea of the the Mothman cryptid and everybody ran in their own direction with it!

I thought Jason Paulos' "Fair Warning" was really well illustrated and interesting, Ray Mackay and Mike Hoffman's "The Moth and the Flame" was an interesting adventure horror story, and that Mike Hoffman's "The Sign" was a perfect example of trippy horror comics. I gotta ask – what is the meaning behind the sign? Where does that come from?

Can any of us really ever know what the Mothman was? Cause I looked it up, there were real sightings of some giant moth-like creature in Point Pleasant West Virginia and "Moth and the Flame" is set in Crodel National Park which sounds a lot like an actual park in Point Pleasant! What's up with that? Do you and the Eyrie Cohorts believe in the Mothman? I'm open to such a creatures existence, but what do y'all think?
Sincerely,
David Jameson, Point Pleasant, WV

We wouldn't necessarily ask anyone to "believe" in the Mothman, but probably you shouldn't automatically disbelieve it either! Are all those folks out there lying? Maybe not...

Dear Eyrie Magazine,
Long time reader first time writer Frank Dellamorte here. I've been reading Eyrie since #16 when your "The Experiments Of Henry Ward" story caught my attention. I liked the fun mad-science-zombie story and was creeped out by how evil Henry Ward was, he's like if Doctor Frankenstein hadn't learned his lesson!

I didn't expect to see him again BUT after your full-length werewolf story in issue nineteen by Mike Hoffman and Don Marquez I was curious – will any of

GRUESOME GREETINGS TO YOU DEAR READER, AND WELCOME EYRIE #20! I'M KNOWN AROU HERE AS "THE FEARLEADER" A DON'T YOU FORGET IT, PUNK! I MADE A COZY DEAL WITH V HOFFMAN TO HOST THIS CRUM HORROR MAG BUT HONESTLY T EXPOSURE I WAS PROMISED AIN'T EXACTLY FORTHCOMING! MAYBE IT'S TIME TO FREAK AND GO BALLISTIC ON HIS ASS YOU TELL ME, EYRIE-ITE!

Eyrie's stories be ongoing or have follow-ups? I'd love to see "The Return of Henry Ward" or some kind of a follow up to "The Werewolf Chronicles". But most of all, I just wanna read more Eyrie Magazine!
Keep up the great work!
Franklin Dellamorte Boston, MA

Thanks for your enthusiasm, and yes, there could feasibly be some follow-up tales in future issues, but only if there's some legitimate new angle to explore.

Hey Mike,
Greetings from up North, and yes, Eyrie has fans above the American Border! I enjoy reading your horror comics in my igloo after a long day of playing hockey. I've read most of your comics (give or take an issue or two) but my favourite has got to be Eyrie #7, the one with the ghost girl on the moose on the cover. It scratched that itch all Canadians feel to have The Great White North's stories told!

I have to ask - Would you ever consider doing a Canadian horror issue? We've got lots of scary stories from up here – from the tales of the Wendigo in the Ontario Wilderness to the bog-monsters of the Sunshine Coast, Canada's horror stories seem ripe for adaption!

I was so enamoured with Eyrie #7's cover so I was wondering – is there anywhere I can buy a print of this? I'd love to hang it on my wall inbetween my Wayne Gretzky and Captain Canuck posters.
Can't wait for the next issue!
Harry Wardon, Alberta, Canada

Sure, you can get giant 16x20 prints of all EYRIE cover artworks either on Mike's eBay store hoffmaninternational or via the EYROE Kickstarter campaigns. And, you can request them directly from Mike at email EYRIEmag@gmail.com

Hi Mike,
I discovered your work sometime last year, quite by accident. Since that moment I've absorbed as much as I've been able to find (and afford) — and I'm reading through your Painting Mastery book. It's great.

Trying to work out how to approach this message. Basically, I'm writing because I need to acknowledge something about you. Something that astounds me. I'm an illustrator too (I'm sure many of your fans are) and I work really hard to make things I find acceptable — to actually get the pieces I work on to a satisfying place. The only way I've been able to raise the quality of my own material is by comparison to the great illustrators I admire: I ask myself, does my work cut together with theirs? Does it hold up?

Very often the answer is no, but I aspire to greatness. I try to learn from the ones I love best. I don't think I've ever quite figured it out any one of them completely, whereas...

You: You have totally decoded Frazetta, and I think you deserve immortality for it. What I find so astonishing and admirable (and inspiring!) about what you've achieved is — you didn't robotically "master copy" his portfolio. It's a little bit like you expanded it. Yet: your artworks are your own works, from your own imagination, and you did the thing I've always wanted for my own work — you made yours match (and yes, exceed) the quality of a hero. You willed yourself into a god!

I mean, there have been other attempts, but they all got distracted before they finished school. Even the most well-known students are really doing something altogether different (like the Vallejos). Jeffrey Jones, maybe a little, but it's a little ghostly, a little impressionistic. James Gurney idolized Rockwell — I think he's the only other one I can think of who wanted to know so badly how his idol worked that he reverse-engineered the process and persisted til he got there. But very unlike Mr. "I don't know how I do it" Frazetta, Rockwell actually penned his own extremely thorough "here's exactly how I do it" guides!

I'm fairly good friends with SF-based illustrator N8 van Dyke. His style is very different than ours but, of course, like any sane artist, he worships Frazetta. Recently he revealed to me that he owns a few original pencil sketches of FF (maybe you do, too). They're just sitting in his messy apartment, tucked into a file. I took this picture of one, a character study for "Fire & Ice."

Cover the signature there and this could have come from your portfolio. There's no other artist alive today for whom that is true.

It's really a beautiful thing to behold. And I know it wasn't easy. Don't mistake me: your work is beautiful because you are talented and because you wanted it to look a certain way — and you achieved that. Something many of us chase without satisfaction.

I hope this too-long message comes across as the sheer admiration that it is.
Sincerely,
Kiel Bryant

Thanks Kiel, I can't think of any analysis of my artistic pathway that nailed as many points as you have here! Even though it's getting to the twilight years of my career, it's very meaningful and appreciated. Having said that, if I have life to live over again, it wouldn't be as an artist--BWAHAHA!

Mike,
Dude, You are the Coolest! Your kid-friendly art has adorned my walls every Halloween for over 10 Years...

Every Halloween I hang about 10 of your pieces of Art on my walls. Everyone Loves Them!! This Monster Yoga idea is a Smash!! Fantastic!
Greg Maury

Thanks much Greg, as you may know the Monster University music I've created has been a lot of fun but also a huge disappointment due to Pixar's similarly-named property which came after, which effectively knocked my project off the Internet.

It also hasn't helped that the sales of CDs tanked around the same time I released those albums.

Mike, I found your Monster music on Youtube during my first big inward breath of your work — my five year old son was singing "Kid Frankenstein" all October long.

Hearing that is the the finest reward I've ever received in my long years in this business! VH

Story: Ray MacKay Art: Von Hoffman

Vampires of the Future

by Cosmos Van Helsing CVXXI

Vampires have been with us since the earliest days of our cave-dwelling forebears, and there is little reason to believe that they will not also be here in the far-flung future. Mankind's inability to fully eradicate the Vampire scourge in the Past would seem to bear this out; no matter how decimated the Vampire's populations become, through "drought" or via organized campaigns to destroy him, in true hydrae fashion new individuals relentlessly appear to replace the old.

There is also little reason to expect that Vampires of the future will not take advantage of technological leaps made since our time, for although the garden-variety bloodsuckers of the past have shunned garlic and running water, there is no logical reason assume that they will similarly eschew ion-drives or antimatter fusion. May God, in his partly-infinite wisdom, protect us from such possible scourges of Vampires armed with such awesome machineries!

As Mankind reaches out to the very stars themselves, so might the Vampire accompany him there unbeknownst in his flying steel spires of flame and smoke. Whether stowed away in cargo-holds, or tucked away parastically in the very veins of those crewmen yet to be born, there is as much hope of perpetually stemming the Scarlet Cascade of Vampirism as there is in holding the Ocean in a teacup.

Alien races, should we encounter them in our star-journeys, may also fall victim to the terrestrial plague of Vampiris Hemococcus, should their blood-chemistry be like enough to ours to serve as nourishment. In either case, the appetites of the Vampire are insatiable and open to myriad possible paths of evolution, and as he has adapted to feeding on other animals on Earth besides humans, he may be able to harvest the life-juices of hitherto undiscovered beings on those far worlds we will yet encounter.

On Earth proper, it may come to pass that the Vampire overcomes his father race, the Human, and will keep him forever in a state of perpetual bondage and servitude, much as we keep cattle and livestock today. In point of fact, many of the higher-eschelon officers of the Nazis of WWII were in fact Vampires, and utilized the peculiar advantages of their many prison camps in similar fashion.

The Vampire onslaught, as it exists today and will certainly go on tomorrow, will demand every skill and talent Humanity possesses to hold it at bay as we boldly stride into the mysterious, unknown lands of the Future!

ICE IN THE VEINS

L-LADY AGNIA, I-I CAN FEEL A SLIGHT DAMPNESS ON MY B-BACK!

KADY! GREENLY! LISTEN... I WANT BOTH OF YOU TO TAKE A *DEEP BREATH*, WE ARE *SAFE!* WE ONLY NEED TO REMAIN IN HERE, FOR A FEW MINUTES.

LIKE "SNIF" WOT?

LIKE *WHAT?* LIKE... HOW ABOUT I TELL YOU ABOUT MY LIFE?

Y-YOU SAID THE WATER *COULDN'T* GET IN, YOU DID!

TURN YOUR THOUGHTS TO OTHER THINGS!

BORN IN A RUSSIAN PROVINCE NEITHER OF YOU COULD PROPERLY PRONOUNCE I WAS TOLD *REPEATEDLY* HOW I WAS SERIOUS CHILD. >FEH< WHAT DID I KNOW THIS SERIOUS? I'D ALWAYS BEEN CHILD AND I'D ALWAYS BEEN ME.

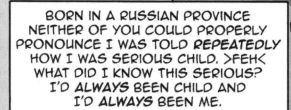

YOU KNOW WHAT *ELSE* I WAS TOLD REPEATEDLY? THAT I WAS BEAUTIFUL.

WHEN NOT MUCH OLDER THAN *YOU*, KADY. I KNEW THE *EXTENTS* A PERSON COULD BE DRIVEN TO BY AN *UNCONQUERABLE LUST* FOR SOMETHING. ONLY *LATER*, TO ETERNAL SHAME, WOULD I DISCOVER *FIRST HAND* THE TRUE LENGTHS SUCH NEEDS COULD LEAD ONE TO.

WHILE NOT *IMPOVERISHED*, MY FAMILY COULD PROVIDE DOWRIES FOR *ONLY* THE OLDEST GIRLS, SO THERE WERE ONLY *TWO* PATHS FOR ME, THE CHURCH OR THE ARTS.

KNOWING THEIR YOUNGEST POSSESSED *BOTH* A SHARP TONGUE AND LONG, SLENDER FINGERS MY PARENTS CHOSE THE LATTER.

Story © Barry Buchanan   Art: Von Hoffman

ONCE AT SEA I WAS A *WOLF* AMONG SHEEP IN A VERY SMALL PASTURE. A FACT THAT MY DEAR, *DEAR* REBECCA *TRIED* AND *TRIED* TO DRIVE INTO MY HEAD!

AGAIN, I HAVE ALWAYS BEEN *AGNIA RUZOMAV* AND A *RUZOMAV* WOULD *NEVER* LET...LET A-A SERVANT *DICTATE* WHAT DAUGHTER OF A NOBLE HOUSE *WOULD* OR *WOULDN'T* DO!

The Scientific and Evolutionary Basis for VAMPIRISM

by Dr. P. Osbert Horrelson, MVS.

The original germ of Vampirism may have indeed come to this world from space; we have no scientific way of ascertaining that fact for certain, but recent genetic studies show unique and apparently foreign nucleotide arrangements in the blood components of Vampiric subjects. Many scientists believe that the likelihood these strains would develop via terrestrial evoutionary pressures is unlikely in the extreme.

The original prototype of the terrestrial vampire may have lurked in tidal-pools of the earliest ages in Earth's history, feeding the parasitic, invading lifeforms in its blood as they reciprocated by keeping the host animal alive in perpetuity. The disease may then have spread rampantly throughout the species population.

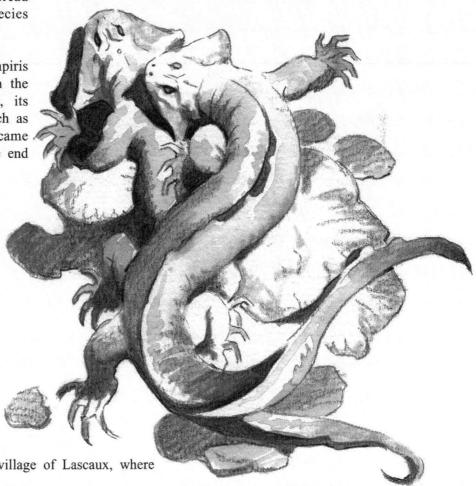

Due to the disease parasite Vampiris Hemococcus' aversion to waves in the ultraviolet parts of the spectrum, its infestation of nocturnal animals such as wolves, rats, owls and bats became increasingly widespread towards the end of the Cretaceous period.

When early Man took shelter in the dank caves of prehistoric Europe, he found other, more persistent threats to his race than the giant cave-bear; the Vampiris-infected bats had been there long before him, and would stay long after he had departed.

The earliest forms of writing make pictorial mention of what could be logically assumed is Vampirism. The original cave-paintings I discovered were unfortunately destroyed during the German occupation of the French village of Lascaux, where these caverns are located.

As man struggled to vault himself out of the Natural World and into the Modern Age, he brought his nocturnal brethren with him. Like the ebb and flow of blood in his veins, his Vampiric counterparts swelled and shrank in number as conflicts between them arose with marked regularity.

Soon, the Vampiric families of the Medieval Age had carved out safe niches for themselves in the aristocracy of Europe, especially in areas around the Black Sea such as Moldavia, Batavia, and Transylvania. "Marriages" were arranged between the races in a effort to improve relations with the peasantry and other Kingships, but as often as not the resultant publicity created the opposite of the desired effect.

The battle between human and vampire raged many long centuries across Europe. Eventually, Vampirism spread to the other continents, the Americas, China, and even Australia, ultimately encircling the globe with a Scarlet Cascade.

Romance by Moonlight

by R. Constance Beatrice

Once upon a Nighttime dreary,
A lad gave a lass a look rather leery;
And as she turned away,
Aloof and in huff,
The boy changed his tune,
Growled grav'ly and gruff:
Dear sister, my goodness,
What eyeballs you have;
What lips, what hairs,
What projections and stuff!
If only you were Wolfen,
Like me, what a thrill--
To gambol and frolic
In bloodthirst and chill!
To this she responded
With quietness and grace;
"Sir Wolf, I am happy,
To be born of this race;
The Vampire, you see,
Is nocturnal too--
Though there we part ways,
And boy, do we do!
What my folks might say, livid,
Should you ask for a date,
Why, they might turn alive
Should I become your mate"
To all this the wolf listened,
Then answered "In truth,
There is no problemmo,
For I'm Vampires too!

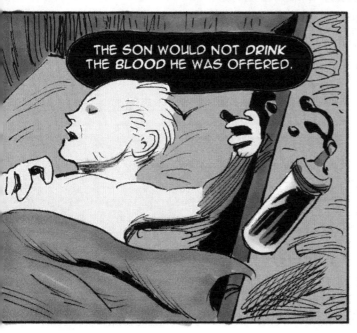

VAMPIRES of the OLD WEST

by Sgt. Abner Darnwell Shooter
Originally published in the New West Times, April 1972

Vampiris Hemococcus rapidly spread worldwide during the European "Small Plague" of the early 1800s, and a few radical ultraviolet-resistant strains migrated to the Americas via shipboard rats, finally reaching and infecting areas of the North American West.

Many stories appear in records from the 1880s in particular, some fanciful, but others clearly rooted in fact. In total, there are over 400 case of overt Vampirism in this period, as the germ was easily transported by cattle and other livestock, the economic mainstays of the Old West, and quickly over long distances by the plentiful horses of the Cowboys.

The first corroborated example of traditional Vampiric activity is written in the town record of Swilville, outside Stank Butte, Colorado. A part-time railroad employee named Homer Jacobson, known locally for keeping pet rodents, apparently wild packrats, as pets, allowing them to live in his clothing and voluminous beard and sleep there as well. It is widely held that these rats were the original source of infection that ultimately eradicated upwards of seventy-five percent of the town's citizens.

Other accounts claim that Homer, as a Vampire, attracted even larger numbers of rats and used them as a fighting force against the normal, still-human population. The rats assaulted the people continously, causing a mass exodus from Swillville to Oregon, but

Continued next page...

but the flight was to no avail as the rats followed by night.

Finally, in the Winter of 1881, Homer Jacobson was run through with a short section of steel rail by an unnamed vagrant who, fearing a murder charge, fled the scene. Once the Master Vampire Jacobson died, his leaderless vampire underlings' morale was destroyed and a special team of Federal Marshals closed in to finish the job, and the reign of terror finally came to a close.

Another well-documented case involves the oddly named snake-oil merchant turned mortician Rilk Morbo, who operated the latter business out of the town of Sleer City, Idaho. His talent for extravagant funerals enabled him to openly deal in coffins, to more or less continuously work with graves and travel about with marias containing what the townsfolk believed were inanimate corpses.

By October in 1877, almost everyone in the town had experienced an attack and most had been drained of large quantities of blood, leaving then mainly pale, weak and largely defenseless. Morbo actually recruited as full-fledged vampires only those he needed as agents, and kept the rest of the populace for feeding purposes.

Eventually, as the supply of blood dwindled and the numbers of Vampires grew, Rilk and his ilk resorted to horsethieving to restock their larder, which lasted several more months until all the horses in the area had either died or become vampiric.

Finally, reduced to feeding on rodents and local pets, the Vampire Mortician of Sleer City began buying advertisements in Eastern newspapers in an attempt to entice new victims to travel to Idaho, but as the same tactic had already been used by several other Western towns overcome by Vampirism, these announcements were easily spotted by the authorities. Within three days, a large force of specially armed and trained militia descended on Sleer.

The ensuing battles are unique in several respects; firstly, for the use of a modified gatling gun, re-tooled and uniquely equipped to fire sharpened wooden projectiles; and secondly, for the clever but ultimately futile campaign of the town's nocturnal mortician to garner some pity from the rest of the nation by writing letters to various politicians begging for mercy as he and his fellows were in hiding in the labyrinthine foothills of North Chester county.

These communiques failed to create an atmosphere of sympathy towards Vampires in a country already

nigh-overcome with the plague, and Morbo's laments largely fell upon deaf ears, except in the case of one Ilsa Montagna, a Cincinnati romance-columnist who subsequently authored numerous pieces decrying the cruelties of the human forces and arguing for a separate statehood of Vampires, specifically in the Swedish community of Ruudolki in Kansas, who she claimed had volunteered their town to set an example, but whose mayor denied making such an offer.

After 376 recorded deaths and tremendous loss of farm livestock, not to mention the too-numerous dogs and cats of Sleer City, Rilk and his cohorts were finally flushed from their hideout as a new contingent of Marshalls diverted a nearby river to run through the protective ravines, and the vampires' natural dread of running water sent them scampering away, directly into the lethal fire of eighteen specially-constructed stake-firing weapons.

The following March, the few surviving citizens of Sleer City erected a memorial to their dead fellows. The statue depicts a wild horse trampling a reclining and stovepipe-hatted Rilk Morbo, whose memory should forever live in the minds of Sleerians old and new as they ponder its bold inscription cursing him as "The Man Who Sucked A Town Dry".

THE ROGUES GALLERY OF VAMPIRES

LILITH VLADIMIROV

Originally a Mail-order bride from the Ukraine, the lovely *Lilith Valdimirov* escaped the crushing poverty of a collapsing Soviet empire to build some degree of fame on the late-night talk-show circuit via a modernized vaudeville act, involving stunts such as sucking blood out of turnips, and by wearing outfits made of human skin, and sporting accents like rat-skull earrings with an evening bag made from sow's ears. Recently embarking on a singing career, she and her boyfriend/manager Lyle Bloodless have expressed interest in transporting their bizarre nightclub act to Las Vegas in the hopes of becoming the house entertainers at a major Casino there.

BATSON BELFRIES

One of the lesser demons (known as "Moose") on the seventh level of Hell, *Batson Belfries* was previously a celebrated television executive as director and producer of the popular "true cop" program called "BUSTED!". When asked by a documentary filmmaker why he didn't try making less violent T.V. fare in light of several recent gun incidents in kindergartens around the country, the 66-year old director commented that "I wouldn't know how to make a program like that". "BUSTED!" was riding high in the ratings that week, but almost immediately after making the untoward statement Belfries fell to the floor in the throes of a massive, fatal heart attack.

KNUCKLES CORPUSCI

A bad kid from the start, Corpusci got into trouble for truancy, theft, loitering, and cruelty to animals before he was seven. When an opportunity to join a local Brooklyn gang presented itself, "Knuckles" (real name: Costa) eagerly knifed the top man and took his place as leader of the "Crimson Gougers". After an elderly aunt from the old country paid an extended visit to the Corpusci home, the youngest boy Costa was seen only after dark and ate only blood-raw meat. Then, in the Great Gang War of 1952, The Gougers suffered crushing defeats during rumbles with the invading "Neighborhoodlums". These usurpers, discovering that Corpusci's Gougers were all converts to Vampirism, attacked stealthily by day and completely "staked" out their new territory. Corpusci was fatally punctured while napping inside an abandonded boiler.

GERTRUDE HROLF

"Old Gertie" not only has the distinction of being one of the most fantastically horrific-looking women in the world, surpassing even the "Mule Girl" of a 1940s carnival sideshow in pure, naked ugliness, but she also has been married for 347 years to one of the best-known Undeaders of all, Clyde R. Nosferatu himself. Being "Mrs. Nosferatu" has opened many doors for Gertrude, but even more can be heard slamming shut once a brief look at her horrendous puss is had. It's said that in spite of her appearance, she has a heart of gold, which we sincerely hope will never get "staked". Go Gertie!

HECTOR WHISNANT

Born in 1888 as the illegitimate offspring of a Spanish nobleman and an Irish peasant girl, a young Hector found work with a travelling caravan show. He was able, due to his diminutive height, to gain entry into places full-sized persons could not, and thus was born a career unlike any other in the History of Criminology. Hector, while "casing" an abandoned mansion in Shropshire England with several Gypsy companions, was bitten by a *Vampiris Hemococcus* infected hound, itself a victim of Count Dracula himself almost 25 years previously. Hector "died" from the bite wound, only to be resurrected as the World's only Dwarf Vampire cat burglar.

DONALD KERBLOOIE

Kerblooie led the British rock group "The Rodents" in the early 1970s before abandoning them to embark on a permanent binge of costume-changes and trendy image switcheroos. Rick Monsoon, who'd put old Donald on the map musically in the first place, never got a penny for his invaluable musical contributions to those first 11 hit Rodents albums. Since that time, Kerblooie has made a habit of grossly underpaying his musicians and tour personnel, and couldn't be bothered to attend the funeral of the original Rodents bassist, Bernie Gripplestone. Donald Kerblooie epitomizes the old Vampire adage "Suck 'em dry, them move on to the next neck".

WALLY FONTAYNE

This clever fellow has absolutely perfected the art of imitating a corpse, to the degree that he's often totally overlooked in vampire investigations. Witnesses naturally assume he's a victim, but he's just as likely to get up and walk away when no one's looking. In spite of his withered frame and beef-jerky muscles, Wally is an extremely dangerous adversary when cornered.

TABITHA TRUESDALE

Commonly referred to as the "Typhoid Mary of Vampirism", Tabby's not only a highly infectious carrier of *Vampiris Hemococcus*, but also totes a melange of very hip, contemporary STDs, most of which were gotten through contact with patrons of New York City "Goth" clubs. She's discovered that spoiled urbanite kids who wear all black are highly receptive to dangerous, risque nocturnal activities such as blood-drinking and devil worship. But, it's way too late for them by the time they discover that this vampire's the real McCoy.

URBANA KELSO

A new recruit, Urbana got infected with Vampirism during a Peace Corps trip to Botswanaland, probably from eating raw human flesh when her group was lost without provisions in the jungle for six weeks. In 1977, she ate her way back to the U.S. in on a Swedish tramp steamer called "The Nightingale", arriving as the only "living" passenger. An odd vampire specimen, Ms. Kelso believes to this day that she's not actually one of the undead but simply enjoys frequent cannibalism.

FATHER TREACHER

Archibald Z. Treacher impersonated a Roman Catholic priest for some 27 years in a small town outside Bellingham, Washington, in the early 1920s. Using the confession as a way to gain the trust of potential victims, he had converted most of the town to Vampirism by the time vigilantes invaded the town and gang-staked him.

JEB COUSTEAU

Often attempting to pass himself off as the twin brother of French Oceanographer Jacques Cousteau, citizens of Jeb's home stomping-grounds of Homassassa Springs Florida have long since grown wise to that ruse, forcing this notoriously unemployed vagrant to feed mainly on migrating sea-cows or "manatees", which he hunts in a little home-made boat. To avoid suspicion or being recognized as a vampire, Jeb removed his vampire fangs many years ago with a pair of fishook pliers, fashioning a wooden replacement pair which he keeps handy and inserts when needed.

LANCE LIPPMANN

Weighing in at 350+ pounds, Lance is certainly one of the largest Vampires on record, and he's got an appetite to match. He's been known to drain whole posses, a soccer team, and, in a much-publicized smorgasbord, 18 members of the U.N. who were out for a stroll. He was, however, thwarted when he attempted to dive from the rafters onto the New York City Ballet company; the dancers saw Lance coming, and being mainly from "The Old Country", quickly formed the shape of a cross on the stage with their bodies. Lance dodged, but was fatally impaled on a hot Klieg light.

COUNT VON TORPOROV

Alexei Von Torporov became one of the undead in 1941 after being bitten by an infected sloth in South America. Perhaps as a result of some inter-species affinity, the Count now enjoys hanging upside down and is a very slow mover indeed. In spite of this, he's quite a ladies man and has been married over seventy times. Rumor has it that his long eyelashes are irresistable to women.

BRIANA KOLDSLABECI

Briana came to the U.S. as part of a Romanian Olympic team in 1972, and after marrying a distant relative and descendant of Count Dracula himself has stayed on ever since. She employs the odd (for a vampire) practice of never drinking from the neck; only from a glass cup or gold chalice. She's quite the entertainer also, giving grand parties for the Undead in her palatial home in Salt Lake City. Should you be lucky enough to attend one of these soires, you're likely to dine on live mice and blood sausage, all washed down with carbonated plasma.

ARE YOU READY FOR YOUR BLIND DATE...

...WITH EYRIE?

ARE YOU ALWAYS HURRYING...

...TO GET ISSUES OF EYRIE?

ALL THE BEAUTIFUL PEOPLE READ EYRIE!

EYRIE READERS ARE LOYAL TO THE END!

"THE HEADSMAN" FINE ART PRINT!

18X24 ON HEAVY MATTE PAPER W/FREE USA SHIPPING!
Mailed rolled in tube, $29.95 each via PayPal to:
HoffmanIntl@hotmail.com Use Code: HDSMP

30 Mike Hoffman Comics!

The Complete Collection!

"THE HALLOWEEN TREE"

Two magnificently mad images created in the lab by Von Hoffman! Bwa-ha-ha!

A MERE $75 EACH!

A putrid pair of gigantic 18x24 stretched canvas prints to adorn your horrid walls this October!

"THE GHOST HOUSE"

W/ FREE US SHIPPING!

5 Mike Hoffman Art Books!!

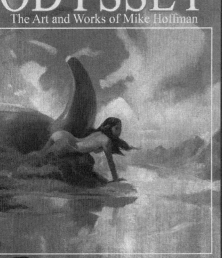

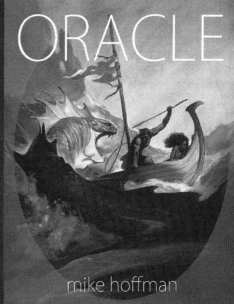
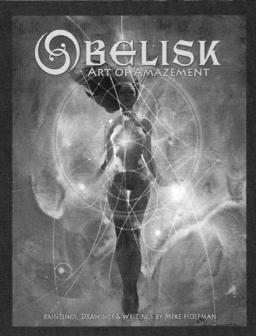
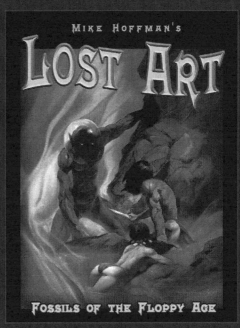

The Complete Library!

Exploratory, adventurous, iconic, humorous, horrific, exotic and erotic masterful artworks 5 books collecting decades of Artistic evolution! All 5 Volumes $120

EYRIE BACK ISSUES AVAILABLE NOW!

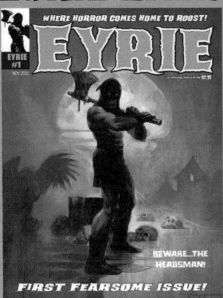

FIRST FEARSOME ISSUE!

SECOND SCARY ISSUE!

3RD BLOODTHIRSTY ISSUE!

FOURTH FEARSOME ISSUE!

FIFTH FRIGHTFUL ISSUE!

SIXTH SPECTACULAR ISSUE!

SEVENTH SPECTRAL ISSUE!

EIGHTH INCREDIBLE ISSUE!

COMPLETE YOUR COLLECTION OF EYRIE MAGAZINES AT MIKEHOFFMAN.COM/EYRIE

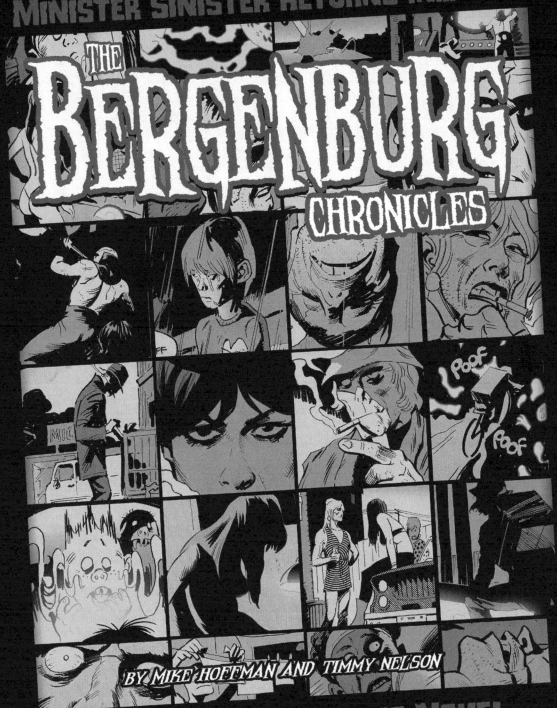

Carmilla #1
MAY 2021

CARMILLA
THE VAMPIRESS

A VON HOFFMAN PUBLICATION $7.95

THE ORIGINAL & DEADLIEST FEMME FATALE OF ALL!

FIRST FRIGHTFUL ISSUE!

3 Mike Hoffman Illustration Books!!

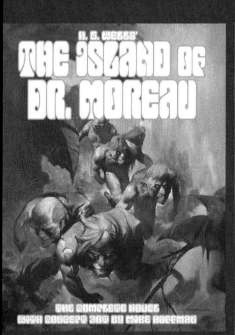
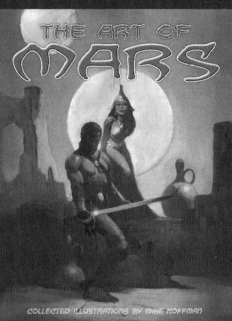

Myths, Legends & Fantasy!

3 Mike Hoffman Ink Art Books!

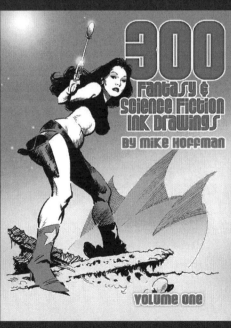
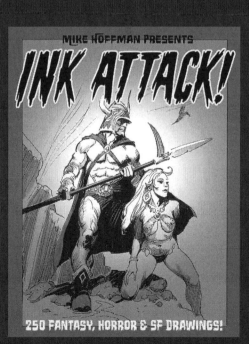

700 Fabulous Drawings in ALL!

3 Von Hoffman Music Albums!

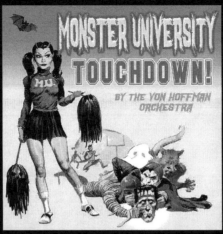
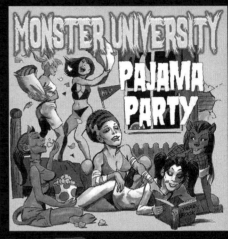

39 Monstrous Songs in All!

3 Mike Hoffman Ink Art Books!

700 Fabulous Drawings in ALL!

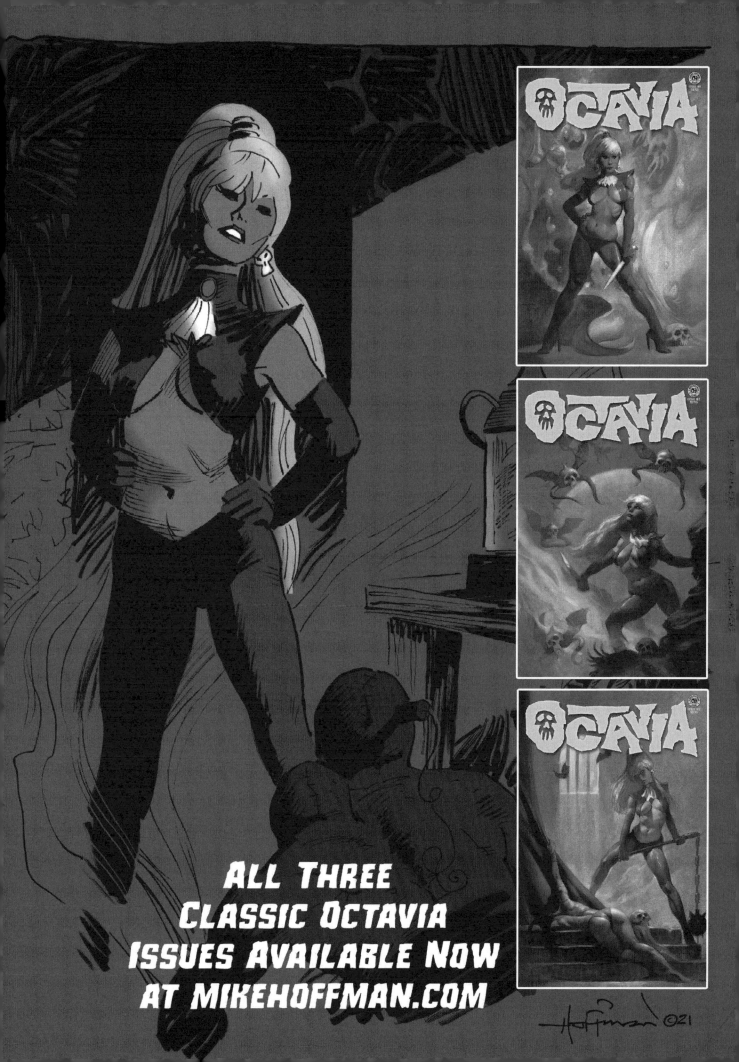

4 Fantastic Hoffman Art Journals!

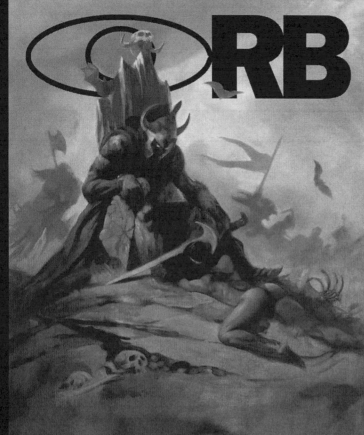

1100 pages total of Unseen Art, Articles, Essays & more!

9 Mike Hoffman Sketchbooks!

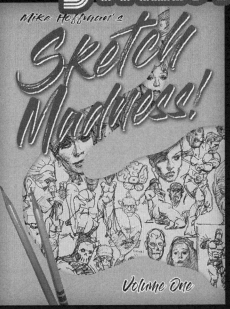
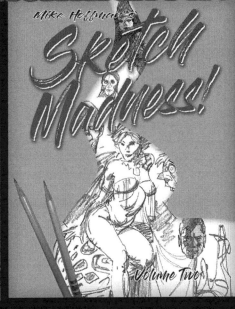
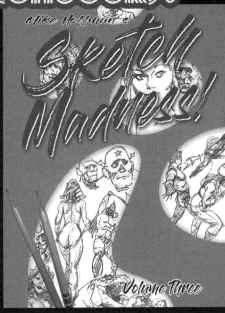

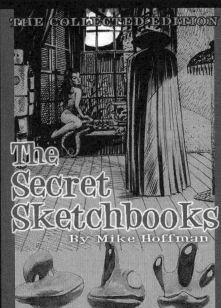
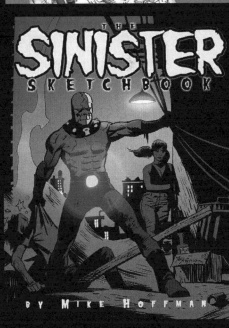
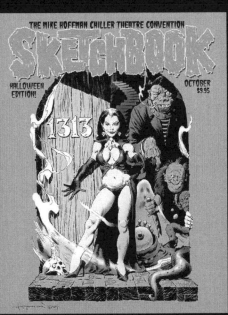

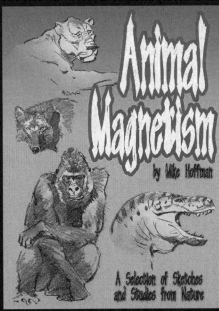

750 Pages Total!

ALL THE GROOVIEST MONSTERS DIG EYRIE!

NOT AVAILABLE IN STORES!

ARE YOU ALWAYS HURRYING...

...TO GET ISSUES OF EYRIE?

Made in the USA
Columbia, SC
12 July 2024

bc0ad6bb-c6a7-44fd-b2db-60160d6bc07eR01